Public Forum Debate

Jason Kline

New York

I would like to thank Scott Wunn of the NFL for giving me the opportunity to write this book and to serve the NFL in other capacities. Also, my thanks to numerous colleagues for their guidance and to my Public Forum students for their enthusiasm and inspiration.

Published in 2007 by The Rosen Publishing Group, Inc.
29 East 21st Street, New York, NY 10010

First Edition

Library of Congress Cataloging-in-Publication Data

Kline, Jason.
  Public forum debate / Jason Kline.
    p. cm. — (The National Forensic League library of public speaking and debate)
  Includes bibliographical references and index.
  ISBN-13: 978-1-4042-1027-1
  ISBN-10: 1-4042-1027-X (library binding)
  1. Debates and debating. I. National Forensic League (U.S.) II. Title.
  PN4181.K56 2007
  808.53--dc22
                              2006030091

Manufactured in the United States of America

The National Forensic League Honor Society promotes secondary school speech and debate activities and interscholastic competition as a means to develop a student's lifelong skills and values, as well as the public's awareness of the value of speech, debate, and communication education.

The organization serves as the central agent for coordination and facilitation of:

- heightened public awareness of the value of speech communication skills;
- development of educational initiatives for student and teacher training;
- excellence in interscholastic competition;
- the promotion of honor society ideals.

As an organization, the National Forensic League embraces diversity, interconnection, and visionary leadership. The National Forensic League empowers students to become effective communicators, ethical individuals, critical thinkers, and leaders in a democratic society.

To learn more about starting a National Forensic League or National Junior Forensic League program at the middle or high school level, or to locate more resources on speech and/or debate, please contact National Forensic League, 125 Watson Street, Ripon, WI 54971, (920) 748-6206, or visit our Web site at **www.nflonline.org**.

Contents

Chapter 1

Introducing Public Forum Debate

You are about to read about a new and exciting forensic debate event. Public Forum Debate, also known as Controversy or Crossfire Debate, requires all the skills necessary for forensic speech events and the research and argumentation skills needed for debate. Public Forum Debate is less formal than other forms of debate and uses less special language. It's meant to be audience friendly, so it's conducted in language the average person would understand. It's lively and requires debaters to be able to think on their feet. Many people consider Public Forum to be the most fun and challenging of the National Forensic League (NFL) debate events.

Public Forum Debate was added to the NFL National Speech Tournament as a trial event in 2003. The event quickly became very popular and was made official in 2004. Speech and debate tournaments across the country offer Public Forum Debate. Public Forum Debate is sometimes referred to as Ted Turner Debate because its style resembles that of *Crossfire*, a news program on CNN founded by Ted Turner.

What Is Public Forum Debate?

The best thing about Public Forum is its simplicity. Public Forum Debate is a more organized way of doing what we already do! Most of us "debate" over small things every day. For example, whenever you disagree with your parents over your curfew or tell your friends that the latest X-Men movie is the best yet, you already know that you have to give reasons for your argument.

These students are discussing—or informally debating—a topic between classes.

7

The idea behind Public Forum is that debate should be clear and understandable to a "common" or community audience. The topics, or debate resolutions, are based on current issues. Debate events such as Policy Debate and Lincoln-Douglas Debate can be very complicated to listeners. They require language and speaking styles that may not be familiar to many people. Public Forum, on the other hand, was created for the purpose of making debate interesting and enjoyable for all audiences.

According to former NFL National Secretary James Copeland, the purpose of Public Forum Debate is to convince people your side is the best side of the debate. This requires debaters to research topics, prepare compelling arguments, and skillfully present their case. When you debate in public, you must be understandable to the audience.

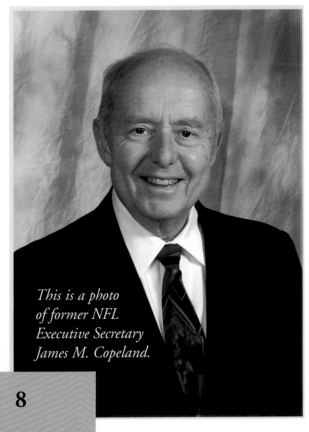

This is a photo of former NFL Executive Secretary James M. Copeland.

In Public Forum Debate, you must be prepared to argue both sides of a controversial issue, since you won't know in advance what side of the debate you'll be on. You must also be able to provide evidence to support your arguments. You must be able to think on your feet. You must do all these things while speaking clearly and presenting yourself well.

A judge serves as the moderator of the debate. The judge evaluates and awards points to

8

the competitors. The judge declares a winner at the end of the round and submits a written ballot with comments and suggestions about the decision.

Throughout this book, we'll examine the method of Public Forum Debate. We'll discuss how to approach topics, arguments, and opponents. Together, we'll find a positive approach to success in Public Forum Debate.

The Rules of Public Forum Debate

Before we get into the "how-to" of Public Forum Debate, we should look at the rules of the event. In order to compete, you must have a partner. Public Forum is a team event. Each debate is also moderated by an adult, who is the judge.

Each debate starts with a resolution. A resolution is a statement that says what you will be debating. An example of a Public Forum Debate resolution might be:

> *Resolved: That the United States government should reduce spending on the military.*

In a debate round, there will be a pro team and a con team. The pro team is in favor of the resolution; the con team is against it. But how do you know which side you will be on? Before you begin the round of debate, a member of one team will toss a coin into the air and a member of the other team will call heads or tails. The winner of the coin toss then gets to decide one of two things:

> 1. Whether to take the pro or con side of the resolution.
> or
> 2. Whether to go first or second in the round.

The team that loses the coin toss then gets to make the choice in the remaining option. Let's say that you win the coin toss. If you choose to take the pro side, then your opponents get to decide whether they will speak first or second in the round. Each team also decides which partner will speak first and which will speak second.

Once the sides of the debate and the speaking order are set, the round will begin. The team who chose to speak first will deliver a 4-minute speech giving arguments for or against the resolution, depending on which side they are on. This is followed by a 4-minute speech from the other team giving the arguments for their side. This second speaker may also speak against arguments presented by the first speaker. After both sides have given their speeches, the speakers then engage in "crossfire" for 3 minutes. Crossfire is the only time during a debate round where Public Forum debaters argue directly with each other. During the 3-minute crossfire, the previous speakers ask questions of each other and answer accordingly.

At the end of the first crossfire, each team will again give a 4-minute speech. The second speaker from each team delivers this speech. Once again, the team speaking first in the opening round speaks first in the second round. After the speeches, the speakers follow the same procedure as the first speakers and crossfire for 3 minutes.

At the completion of this crossfire, the first speakers from each team then get 2 minutes to deliver a "Summary Speech." This speech includes a restatement of their case and arguments against what their opponent has presented. The team who chose to speak first in the coin toss again speaks first, followed by the speaker from the second team. After these Summary Speeches, there is the "Grand Crossfire." In this part of the debate, all four debaters ask and answer questions of each other for 3 minutes. The Grand Crossfire is begun by the speaker who gave the first Summary Speech.

At the completion of the Grand Crossfire, each team's second speaker gives a 1-minute "Final Focus" speech explaining why they believe their team has won the round. The Final Focus speech cannot contain any new arguments.

In Public Forum Debate, each team also has 2 minutes of preparation time to use during the debate. Teams can use it at any time during the round, before any of their speeches. The judge keeps track of each team's time used and time remaining. Teams might use preparation time to work on their arguments or discuss the direction of the debate.

Debating Guidelines

Successful debating requires students to present themselves professionally. Here are some important guidelines to follow:

1. Do not comment or distract your opponents while they are speaking.
2. Keep your voice low during preparation time.
3. Be polite to your judge and opponents before, during, and after the round.
4. Never make up evidence.
5. Be on time (or early) for your rounds.
6. Follow all posted tournament rules.

Keep in mind that how you conduct yourself is a deciding factor in your success in all debate events, including Public Forum Debate.

Chapter 2

Forming a Public Forum Team

Some people think they would make good debaters because they are good at "arguing." Debate is more about listening and responding rather than simply disagreeing. Think about an argument you have had with someone in the past. How much listening did you do? Did you acknowledge what the other person said and then reply? In debate, it is important to give reasons for or against what your opponent says and not simply disagree. To present your point of view, and to challenge your opponent's points, you must be a good listener.

One difficulty that debate poses to new competitors is that it requires skills that they may not possess naturally. When challenged, a natural reaction is to "fight back," often without much thought. In Public Forum Debate, however, we learn to defend a challenge by being an engaged listener. An engaged listener is someone who thinks as they listen, creating responses to an opponent's arguments, and predicting what an opponent may say next.

Picking a Partner

Public Forum Debate is a team event. A major task of any debater is to partner with someone they are comfortable with and can work with. Debate partners should have skills that complement each other. Remember, in debate you want a partner who is a good listener.

For a Public Debate partner, you want someone who is also:

- a clear speaker
- a focused thinker
- a hard worker
- organized
- open to critical evaluation

All these characteristics strengthen with practice and competition. The last characteristic—being open to critical evaluation—is especially important for a debater. In practice, evaluation from a debate coach or teacher can provide helpful guidance. In competition, written comments from the judge can provide valuable feedback for sharpening your critical thinking and communication skills. As an effective debater, you should be receptive to these valuable forms of critical evaluation.

This young man is relaxed and focused as he takes part in a debate.

13

Team Responsibilities

Each member of a Public Forum Debate team has specific tasks.

Speaker One:
- Present the first speech.
- Conduct the first crossfire.
- Summarize the debate.
- Participate in the Grand Crossfire.
- Aid partner in rebuttal and Final Focus.

Speaker Two:
- Aid the first speaker in the first crossfire.
- Present the first rebuttal.
- Conduct the second crossfire.
- Participate in the Grand Crossfire.
- Deliver the Final Focus.

The first speaker must present a very good first case, while the second speaker has to be able to argue persuasively at the end of the debate. The person who is best at speaking without preparation should probably be the second speaker, although both partners will have to develop this skill.

It is important to recognize that when you first begin to debate, you may not be outstanding at all these duties. Debate takes a lot of practice. You might discover after a few months of practice and competition that you are much better at speaking without a lot of notes than you were at first. Adaptation is very important in debate. This means that during a debate round, you must be able to adjust to the judges, your audience, and most especially your opponents.

You may also find as you gain experience that you might benefit from changing your approach or even your role on the team. Be open-minded!

Making It Work

You will not become a good debater through natural skill alone. Practice really does make perfect in debate.

Partners should establish a routine when preparing for a tournament. Team members should work both individually and together in order to be successful. It is wise to divide research duties so that you can examine different material. Remember, in Public Forum Debate, you do not know

Team members practice their debate techniques.

15

which side of the debate you will be on until you get there. Each partner can research evidence to both support and refute the resolution. Keep in mind, no matter which side of the debate you end up on, your research will help you to state your case and disprove your opponent's. After each partner has researched and written out cases separately, partners should discuss their research and writing, focusing on important points. Prior to a competition, partners should plan on several practice rounds. Other students in a school can assist with these "trial runs" before a competition. Coaches can review the practice rounds, and partners and coaches can work together on improving debate skills.

To make your team work, you must emphasize competition and practice. Learning to divide up your work will not only save you time, but also make you more competitive. Good teamwork will take you far.

Partners review their research before beginning a debate.

Chapter 3

Resolution Analysis

Each month during the school year, the National Forensic League releases a Public Forum Debate resolution. The resolution is the topic for debate for all Public Forum Debate tournaments for the following month. The resolutions are written by a small group of debate coaches and used in tournaments nationwide.

Resolutions deal with topics of national concern. For example, past topics have included:

1. A just government should provide health care to its citizens.

2. In matters of collecting military intelligence, the ends justify the means.

3. The pursuit of scientific knowledge ought to be limited by a concern for societal good.

The debate resolution is written as a statement. In a debate round, the resolution is supported by the pro team and is refuted by the con team.

Types of Resolutions

There are three types of resolutions generally used in Public Forum Debate: factual, policy, and philosophical. All three are similar in organization but differ in other ways. While factual and policy resolutions deal with reality, philosophical resolutions involve comparing ideal situations.

How to Approach a Resolution

Here is an example of a National Forensic League policy resolution:

Resolved: Use of a cell phone should be prohibited while operating a motor vehicle.

Do you think using a cell phone while driving is a safety hazard?

After reading a resolution, you should identify and examine its parts. Topic analysis will help you do this. Topic analysis requires answers to three basic questions:

1. Who is the actor or agent of the action?
2. What is the action?
3. What are the conditions of the resolution?

Let's use topic analysis to break down the sample resolution. Who is the actor or agent? The actor or agent is the person, group, or government that must act. In this case, the government is the actor since only it could prohibit cell phone use. Knowing this allows us to limit the debate. If someone tried to argue that we should not prohibit cell phone use because people driving cars will not give up their cell phones, we know that argument is not in the scope of the resolution because we are debating government action. However, the ease of enforcing this issue can be discussed.

Next, we need to determine the action. In this resolution, the action is a prohibition (or ban) on cell phone use while driving. This can be a very tricky part of the resolution. You need to think about all the possible arguments that can be made based on the action. For example, a ban on using cell phones while operating a motor vehicle would require a means of enforcement. The enforcement of such a ban could become a very important issue of debate.

Finally, look at the conditions of the resolution by examining the "measuring words." These are the words that control the situation described in the resolution. In this case, the word "should" is very important. "Should" tells us that we are debating an ideal situation. That we "should" do something conveys the idea that it will improve a situation.

Why is it important to identify the conditions of the resolution? In our example, the words "motor vehicle" convey that the resolution would have a broad interpretation. In other words, it would affect anyone who drives any type of motor vehicle. It would affect *all* drivers and not a limited number. Let's say you are on the con side, arguing that cell phone use while driving should be permitted. If your opponents, as part of their argument, say that the cell phone ban would not apply to truck drivers, you could respond that the wording of the resolution indicates that it would apply to all people operating motor vehicles, which would include truck drivers. Because of good topic analysis, you would win that argument.

These debate partners are using topic analysis to examine a resolution.

21

Minitopic: Topic Analysis

Let's go a bit further with our topic analysis on the sample reso-lution. Have a problem-solving session with your partner. Read the resolution and break it down into words and phrases. Brainstorm what the words and phrases mean and record your ideas. See the sample below.

Resolved: Use of a cell phone should be prohibited while operating a motor vehicle.

use of a cell phone
- talking
- typing messages
- pressing numbers
- reading messages
- checking voicemail

prohibited
- legally forbidden
- punishable
- discouraged

operating a motor vehicle
- driving a passenger vehicle (car, van, bus, etc.)
- driving a truck
- driving a motorcycle
- driving a scooter

Use these ideas to prepare main arguments. Begin with the pro side of the resolution. What will draw a judge into supporting the resolution? The most obvious contention, or point, of this side would be safety. Here are some possible pro arguments:

1. Using cell phones reduces automobile safety by shifting attention from driving.

2. Banning the use of cell phones will reduce driver distractions.

3. Banning the use of cell phones will increase attention to driving.

4. Banning the use of cell phones will protect other drivers.

5. Banning the use of cell phones will decrease insurance costs.

6. Banning the use of cell phones will reduce how much the government spends on emergency services.

There may also be pro arguments that do not deal with safety issues:

1. Banning the use of cell phones will decrease people's reliance on them.

2. Banning the use of cell phones will allow for privacy and peace.

3. Banning the use of cell phones will reduce the cost of cell phone calls.

The con side of the resolution can deal with issues of freedom and the problems the resolution might cause. Here are some possible arguments:

1. There is no evidence that using cell phones while driving causes accidents.

2. Cell phones allow for quicker contact of emergency workers in case of an accident.

3. Resolution forces police to monitor too much on the road.

4. Resolution bans the use of all forms of cell phones (including hands-free phones).

5. Resolution harms personal freedom of choice.

Remember, brainstorming is a very important first step. However, these arguments are meaningless if you have nothing to back them up. This leads to the next step in the predebate process—researching and finding evidence that supports the positions.

Chapter 4

Researching the Resolution

In order to persuade an audience that your position is correct and your opponent's is not, you must have evidence to back up your position. Anyone can make a statement, but evidence makes it more than just your opinion.

Researching for Public Forum Debate is sometimes easier than for other forms of debate. Policy Debate requires a great deal of library time, and Lincoln-Douglas Debate calls for considerable reading and complex understanding of philosophy. Public Forum research, on the other hand, is done primarily on the Internet.

The primary tools for Public Forum research are a computer and a printer. Most resolutions will deal with policy and factual issues. Research comes from magazines, newspapers, and think tanks. Where should you begin?

Debate partners use the Internet to check and collect information.

Internet research allows you to search for specific information without having to read entire publications. Online Web sites, such as Wikipedia, can be very useful Internet tools. Wikipedia—located at en.wikipedia.org—is a free online encyclopedia that is written by users. Although there is some controversy about whether its content is biased, you can use Wikipedia, or other online sites, as a starting point in the research process.

A search engine is an Internet site that lets you search millions of Web sites for specific terms. Some excellent search engines are Google (www.google.com), Yahoo (www.yahoo.com), and Ask (www.ask.com). When using a search engine, look for more than one string of information. A string of information is a series of words or phrases that tells the search engine what to look for. For example, when researching the expenses involved with the Kyoto Protocol (an international treaty dealing with climate change), the first string you enter will probably be "Kyoto Protocol." This will call up Web sites that contain those words. Many of these sites, however, may not be useful for your specific purpose. Narrow your search by adding more specific details to your entry. Typing in "Kyoto Protocol and costs" will yield Web sites more focused on the particular details you want.

Search engines are excellent tools for finding up-to-date research. To use them properly requires some work. Research webbing is a great way to find information. Webbing involves using research to find more research. Use terms and names in articles previously found as search strings. For example, put the name of a scientist who argues that the Kyoto Protocol is beneficial to Earth on a first search. If you put his name into a new search, with added information, you may find ten new articles. As you read and locate additional information regarding the costs of carrying out international climate control, continue introducing words and phrases to narrow your search.

Using Research

Once you have located information, you must read it carefully to understand its significance for your arguments. Reading for understanding is an important skill debaters must develop.

Research material will often contain summaries that give the main points of an article or publication. Tables of contents identify where to locate information in a publication. Locate the facts and evidence you need and print out copies of the material. Highlight or underline key information that is important to your arguments.

Organizing the material is important to the focus of the round. A major

Creating a fact sheet of important research can help you organize and focus your thoughts.

organization tool is a summary sheet of your important findings called a fact sheet. A fact sheet helps you to write out cases. It is also a valuable source of reference during the round. Create a fact sheet by listing all the arguments you have developed on both the pro and con sides of the debate. Next, beneath each argument, list the supporting evidence from your research. Summarize the evidence and include a complete citation of the source: author, title, journal name, and publication date. Using the fact sheet, organize the paper copies of research in file folders by side—pro and con—and by argument.

Chapter 5

Writing Your Case

A case is the opening speech of the debate. It is where the arguments in defense of your side of the debate are presented. The case contains definitions of important terms, the main contention or point, arguments, and evidence to support the arguments. The case should do two things: establish what the debate is about and prove that your position is the correct one.

Cases are generally structured in three parts. The **introduction** states the position on the resolution and briefly presents the arguments. The **body** contains the main contentions. The **conclusion** reviews the points and arguments, and refers back to the introduction.

The case is very important in the debate round. Without a solid case, you allow your opponents to determine the direction of the debate. Writing an effective case enables you to stand your ground against your opponents by establishing where the debate is headed.

Framing the Debate

The opening speech of the debate, your case, is the first impression a judge receives. Your goal is to convince the judge your point of view is the correct one. If you do this effectively, the judge should feel compelled to vote for you before hearing your opponent. Of course, once your opponent speaks, the judge may change their mind. It is your task to establish your case and present evidence that cannot be refuted by your opponent. A good case does not guarantee you a win, but a bad case almost always guarantees you a loss.

During a debate round, your goal is to convince the judge that you are right in your contentions. The first way to do this is to frame the debate for the judge. When you frame the debate, you make it clear what is important in the round. It is key to establish burdens of proof at the beginning of the round. A burden of proof is a requirement to prove an argued claim or charge is true. In Public Forum Debate, there is no set burden of proof on either side of the debate. Some resolutions may suggest burdens of proof, but usually the debaters in the round will establish this. Consider this resolution on the rebuilding of New Orleans after Hurricane Katrina:

Resolved: That the federal government should be solely responsible for reconstruction in areas devastated by Hurricane Katrina.

The pro—in support of the federal government being solely responsible—will probably want to establish a burden of proof on the con with regard to finances. Since local and state governments, on their own, could not afford to rebuild, then the con needs to show why the federal government should not offer its funds. The con could place a burden of proof on the pro to show why the

This photo shows the damage done to one home in New Orleans, Louisiana, by Hurricane Katrina.

federal government should be solely responsible for the rebuilding. In doing this, the con and the pro are telling the judge what he should be paying attention to. Of course, you have to convince the judge that your burden of proof is applicable to the round.

Proving Your Case

The next step in Public Forum Debate is to prove your case. If your opponent places a burden of proof on your case, proving the burden will help you win the round by presenting contentions and arguments that support your case. In our example resolution, a contention for the pro side might be that state and local governments cannot handle the reconstruction. That contention must be supported by arguments that prove it to be true. One argument could be that state and local governments in the affected areas did not have enough money in their budgets to provide for the reconstruction.

Remember, arguments only stand when you can uphold them as true. This is where research and evidence come in. In the case of state budgets, a simple piece of evidence you could use would be the number of dollars the

Information on a fact sheet can help to prove and disprove arguments.

state of Louisiana has to spend on reconstruction. If you compare this to the estimated costs of rebuilding, you will have a pretty solid argument and good support for your contention. In your case, make sure you provide a full citation for each piece of evidence you mention.

Generally, it is wise to provide only two or three main contentions in your case. You only have 4 minutes to deliver your initial case. In order to support your contentions thoroughly, do not spread yourself too thin with too many contentions.

It is also wise to build your case in logical order. Your contentions should tie in with each other. You may choose to connect them to a common theme. Write your case so that each contention leads to the next. Ultimately, you want the judge to be persuaded by your arguments. A strong, logical case is the best way to do that.

As you complete your first case, try to identify where your case fits into the outline on page 35. You may have more evidence under some arguments than others. You may also use three arguments rather than two.

Working on an outline can help you format your case in a clear, effective way.

34

Minitopic: Case Structure

Here is a sample outline that shows how a case can be structured. Keep in mind that not all cases will be structured the same way.

I. Introduction
   A. attention-getting story, quotation, or short joke related to topic
   B. statement of your position on the resolution
   C. brief statement of contentions
II. Contentions
   A. contention one
      1. argument A with evidence
      2. argument B with evidence
   B. contention two
      1. argument A with evidence
      2. argument B with evidence
   C. contention three
      1. argument A with evidence
      2. argument B with evidence
III. Conclusion
   A. review contentions
   B. restatement of position
   C. reconnect to introduction

Chapter 6

In the Round

In this chapter, we'll explore what happens in a round of Public Forum Debate. Keep in mind that a fundamental principle of Public Forum Debate is that the debaters communicate and deliver convincing, interesting arguments to a judge and audience of regular people.

You will discover that what occurs in each round will depend on two factors: your personal style of debate and the style of your opponents. Your expressions, gestures, words, and posture all play a very important role in how you are perceived by the audience. Consider each of these factors as you review the following parts of the round.

The Coin Toss

The Public Forum Debate round begins with a coin toss. You will not know which side of the debate you are on or if you are the first or second speaker until after the coin toss. If you win the toss, what should you do? It will depend on the situation.

Do you have a strong opinion about or feel more comfortable with one side of the resolution? Winning the coin toss gives you the opportunity to choose to be either pro or con. Or perhaps you would prefer to decide your speaking position. The first speaker has the advantage of starting the round. The first speaker also gets to ask the first question in each of the three crossfires. This position may help you control the round. The second speaker has the advantage of speaking last, which allows you to have the last word. You and your partner should discuss your coin toss options before every round.

Delivering the First Speech

In the last chapter, we examined what your first speech should contain. Now we will look at the best way to deliver it. It is important that the speech not be read or spoken with mechanical memorization. The delivery should convey knowledge and an understanding of the material. The judge's evaluation will be based not only on content, but also on delivery. You should be as professional as possible.

37

The abbreviation P.E.P. may help:

P–Poised: Stand up tall, and look relaxed and comfortable.

E–Eye contact: Look the judge in the eye from time to time. This gives you a visual connection.

P–Plant your feet: Continuous movement can look like nervousness.

The Crossfire

Crossfire can be the most enjoyable part of Public Forum Debate. According to NFL rules, the crossfire is a back-and-forth question-and-answer period. The only specific rule is that the first question always comes from the competitor on the team that spoke first in the round. Crossfire, however, is not a free-for-all. You can keep it focused and control its direction by adding questions to your statements. Your goal during crossfire should be to get answers about your opponent's case, get them to admit you are correct about an argument, and provide the judge with reasons to vote for you.

Opponents should be courteous and polite, listening as much as they speak. Attacks against an opponent instead of against the ideas they are presenting are considered poor form and are evaluated accordingly by the judge.

Although developing the skills for effective crossfire can be difficult at first, practice and competition strengthen them. Time and experience will help you sharpen and improve your skills.

Rebuttals, Summaries, Grand Crossfire, and Final Focus

The second speech each team gives in a Public Forum round is a 4-minute rebuttal speech. Part of this speech can be prepared before the round. Much of it should

*Looking relaxed and confident as you make
your arguments or question your opponents is
an important debate skill.*

directly refute your opponent's case. Proving them wrong by argument and evidence gives the judge reasons to believe you over your opponent. To help the judge follow your logic, it is important that you state exactly what you are refuting in your opponent's case. This is called signposting. Signposting describes each idea in your speech. In signposting, you make clear your ideas. This helps the audience and the judge understand your argument.

The third speech each team delivers is the Summary Speech. This speech is only 2 minutes in length and requires the arguments in the round be broken down to the most important and relevant ones. In the summary, you will not want to go through everything that has been brought up in the round. Rather, use the time to examine only the most important issues.

Following the Summary Speeches, the Grand Crossfire begins. This crossfire is like the previous two crossfires except that all four debaters take part. In the Grand Crossfire, partners work cooperatively by sharing the time to ask and answer questions.

Final Focus is the last speech in the debate round. This speech is only 1 minute long. In Final Focus, the speakers should choose the issues they feel are most important to the round and present reasons for the judge to select their team as the winner. These reasons are called voters. The Final Focus is the last chance to convince the judge you have won the round.

Note Taking and Preparation Time

There are two important elements of Public Forum Debate to keep in mind. First, it is very important to take organized notes during the debate. Some competitors flow the round while others simply take notes. Flowing involves keeping track of specific arguments made during the round and connecting them on paper to other arguments. No matter how you choose to take notes, be sure to write down as much as you can of what your opponents say.

The second important thing to remember is to make wise use of your preparation time. You will have 2 minutes to use during the round to talk things over with your partner. Many new competitors believe it looks bad to use all their preparation time. That is not true. Use the preparation time as you need it. Do not save it all for the Final Focus. Preparation time is very useful before crossfires, the second speech, and summaries. Clear speaking is a result of clear thinking. Preparation time helps focus your mind.

Developing note-taking techniques you are relaxed and comfortable with is an invaluable forensic skill.

41

Student debaters and coaches work together on how to best present an argument.

Practice Makes Perfect!

An informed, knowledgeable coach is invaluable to debaters. A coach offers advice in outlining and presenting arguments effectively. A coach critically reviews both practice and actual debates, and offers support and analysis.

A Public Forum Debate judge looks for clear-cut interpretations of the resolution; well-explained, related, and established arguments; clarity; organization; and courteous and appropriate conduct by the debaters. Keeping your arguments clear, brief, provable, and to the point will win points and rounds for you in Public Forum Debate.

The more you debate and review your performance, the more comfortable and skilled you will become. Practice, practice, practice is what will help you to become a successful Public Forum Debater!

Glossary

analysis An evaluation of strong points and weak points.

audience A group of listeners or spectators.

citation A quotation of a specific reference.

complement To have strengths that the other one of a pair doesn't.

contention An important point made in a debate.

critical evaluation Exercising careful judgment and analysis.

distract To draw someone's attention away.

evidence The supporting facts that uphold an argument as true.

feedback Information evaluating a performance.

focus The central point of a debate.

frame To arrange arguments and evidence in a way that supports a particular position.

moderator A person who directs a discussion.

National Forensic League The leading honor society and educational resource for teachers, students, administrators, and parents in the field of speech and debate education.

perceive To regard and understand.

rebuttal The process of offering opposing ideas and evidence to refute your opponent's arguments.

receptive To be open and responsive to ideas and suggestions.

relevant Having to do with a specific issue.

think tank An institution, corporation, or group that conducts research about specific issues.

For More Information

National Forensic League
125 Watson Street
P.O. Box 38
Ripon, WI 54971
Phone: (920)748-6206
Web site: www.nflonline.org

National Junior Forensic League
National Forensic League
125 Watson Street
P.O. Box 38
Ripon, WI 54971
Phone: (920)748-6206
Web site:
www.nflonline.org/AboutNFL/NJFL

Web Sites

Due to the changing nature of Internet links, the Rosen Publishing Group, Inc., has developed an online list of Web sites related to the subject of this book. This site is updated regularly. Please use this link to access the list: **http://www.rosenlinks.com/psd/pfde**

For Further Reading

Daley, Patrick, and Michael S. Dahlie. *50 Debate Prompts for Kids*. New York: Scholastic, Inc., 2001.

Davidson, Josephine. *The Middle School Debater*. Bellingham, WA: Right Books Co., Inc. 1997.

Meany, John, and Kate Schuster. *Speak Out! Debate and Public Speaking in the Middle Grades*. New York: IDEA Press, 2005.

Merali, Alim. *Talk the Talk: Speech and Debate Made Easy*. Edmonton, Canada: Gravitas Publishing, 2006.

Bibliography

Averill, Timothy, comp. "NFL Public Forum Debate Steering Committee Minutes." June 15, 2005. Philadelphia, PA: National Forensic League, 2005.

Copeland, James M. "Ted Turner Public Forum Debate: Not Just Another Contest." *Rostrum*, April. 2004. Retrieved July 25, 2006 (http://www.nflonline.org/uploads/Rostrum/pf0404copeland.pdf).

Durkee, John. "Ted Turner Debate: Establishing Theoretical Grounds." *Rostrum*, January. 2003. Retrieved July 25, 2006 (http://www.nflonline.org/uploads/Rostrum/pf0103durkee.pdf).

Hanson, Jim. *NTC's Dictionary of Debate*. Lincolnwood, IL: National Textbook Co., 1991.

Hensley, Dana, and Diana Carlin. *Mastering Competitive Debate*. Topeka, KS: Clark, 1999.

National Forensic League. Public Forum Debate. Ripon, WI: National Forensic League, 2006. Retrieved July 25, 2006. (http://www.nflonline.org/uploads/CoachingResources/PFGuidelines.pdf).

Richards, Jeffery A. *Debating by Doing: Developing Effective Debating Skills: Teacher's Manual*. Chicago, IL: National Textbook Co., 1995.

Wood, Roy V., and Lynn Goodnight. *Strategic Debate*. Lincolnwood, IL: National Textbook Co., 1995.

Index

B
burden(s) of proof, 31, 33

C
case(s), 29, 30, 31, 34, 35
coach(es), 13, 16, 18, 43
con, 9, 18, 21, 25, 29, 31, 33, 37
contention(s), 23, 30, 31, 33, 34, 35
Controversy Debate, 6
critical evaluation, 13
crossfire(s), 10, 14, 37, 38, 40, 41
Crossfire Debate, 6

E
evidence, 8, 11, 16, 25, 26, 29, 30, 33, 34, 35, 38

F
fact sheet, 29
Final Focus, 11, 14, 40, 41
flow(ing), 41
frame, 31

G
Grand Crossfire, 10, 11, 14, 40

I
Internet, 26, 28

J
judge(s), 8, 9, 11, 13, 14, 23, 31, 34, 36, 37, 38, 40, 41, 43

L
Lincoln-Douglas Debate, 8

N
National Forensic League (NFL), 6, 8, 18, 19, 38

P
Policy Debate, 8
preparation time, 11, 41
pro, 9, 10, 18, 23, 24, 29, 31, 33, 37

R
rebuttal, 14, 38
research(ing), 8, 15, 16, 25, 26, 28, 29, 33
resolution(s), 8, 9, 10, 16, 18, 19, 20, 21, 22, 23, 25, 30, 31, 35, 43

S
search engine(s), 28
signposting, 40
string of information, 28
Summary Speech(es), 10, 11, 40

T
team(s), 9, 10, 11, 13, 15, 18, 38, 41
Ted Turner Debate, 6
topic analysis, 20, 21, 22

V
voters, 41

W
webbing, 28

About the Author

Jason Kline is a member of the NFL Public Forum Debate Resolution Wording Committee. Jason, his wife Veronica, and their two dogs live in Fort Mill, South Carolina. He currently teaches and coaches debate at Myers Park High School in Charlotte, North Carolina.

Photo Credits

Cover, p. 39 © Chris Hondros/Getty Images; p. 7 ©PhotoCreate/ Shutterstock; pp. 8, 13, 15, 17, 41, 42 courtesy of the National Forensics League; p. 19 © Galina Barskaya/Shutterstock; p. 21 © Simone van den Berg/Shutterstock; p. 27 © Ana Blazic/Shutterstock; p. 29 © Andres Rodriguez/Shutterstock; p. 32 © Pattie Steib/ Shutterstock; p. 33 © Laurence Gogh/Shutterstock; p. 34 © Gordon Swanson/Shutterstock; p. 37 © Milos Luzanin/Shutterstock.